⟨ **W9-BNU-187**

A Feel Better Book

for Little
Tempers

A FEEL BETTER BOOK
for Little Kids

For Jay and Chris, who love us, tempers and all—HB & LB

To Holly, Leah, and Katie, with my sincerest gratitude—SN-B

Text copyright © 2018 by Magination Press, an imprint of the American Psychological Association. Illustrations copyright © 2018 by Shirley Ng-Benitez. All rights reserved. Except as permitted under the United States Copyright Act of 1976, no part of this publication may be reproduced or distributed in any form or by any means, or stored in a database or retrieval system, without the prior written permission of the publisher.

Published by

MAGINATION PRESS®
American Psychological Association
750 First Street NE
Washington, DC 20002

Magination Press is a registered trademark of the
American Psychological Association.

For more information about our books, including a complete catalog, please write to us, call 1-800-374-2721, or visit our website at www.apa.org/pubs/magination.

Book design by Gwen Grafft
Printed by Lake Book Manufacturing, Inc., Melrose Park, IL

Library of Congress Cataloging-in-Publication Data
Names: Brochmann, Holly, author. | Bowen, Leah, author. |
  Ng-Benitez, Shirley, illustrator.
Title: A feel better book for little tempers / by Holly Brochmann and
  Leah Bowen ; illustrated by Shirley Ng-Benitez.
Description: Washington, DC : Magination Press, American
  Psychological Association, [2018] | Summary: Illustrations and
  simple, rhyming text provide young children with tools for dealing
  with feelings of anger, such as pretending the anger is a baseball
  that can be batted away or breathing deeply.
Identifiers: LCCN 2017024574| ISBN 9781433828171 (hardcover) |
  ISBN 1433828170 (hardcover)
Subjects: | CYAC: Stories in rhyme. | Anger—Fiction.
Classification: LCC PZ8.3.B779 Feb 2018 | DDC [E]—dc23 LC record
available at https://lccn.loc.gov/2017024574

Manufactured in the United States of America
10 9 8 7 6 5 4 3 2 1

A Feel Better Book

for Little Tempers

by Holly Brochmann and Leah Bowen

illustrated by Shirley Ng-Benitez

MAGINATION PRESS · WASHINGTON, DC
American Psychological Association

H ello there my friend,
how are you? Do tell!
Are you happy and calm?
Peaceful and well?

Or is it one of those days
you feel misunderstood?
You're huffy and puffy
and just plain not good.

You wanted it this way.
It went that way instead!
Now your ears are quite hot
and your cheeks are all red.

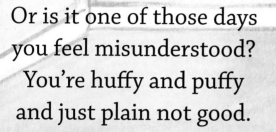

Are you clenching your fists,
is there a frown on your face?
It sounds like a temper
could be the case.

A temper is
what happens
when your
anger's the worst.
You might get so mad
that you think you
could burst!

You try stomping your feet,
maybe a scream or a shout!
You'll do whatever it takes
to get those feelings out.

You may think you'll feel better
by pitching a fit.
But you just get in trouble
when you bite or you hit.

However there's something
important to know.
It's not only you
who has tantrums to throw.

No matter the reason
for why you feel angry,
just remember it's normal.
Even grownups get cranky!

Meow! Meow!

You might not believe this,
it may not seem true,
but it's okay to get mad
if you know what to do!

You just need to learn
some new things to try.
Let's practice together,
just you and I.

Imagine playing baseball
in a uniform and hat.
Pretend your anger is the ball
and your arms are the bat.

Think about how strong you are,
how good it feels to play.
Swing your arms fast
and send that ball far, far away.

There goes your anger!
You can watch it soar!
You're already beginning
to feel better than before.

Then stand up tall
and puff out your chest.
Now you have more power
and your anger has less!

Move!

wiggle

Jiggle

Dance!

Don't stop now,
it's time to get moving.
Try jiggling and wiggling
or dancing and grooving.

Whirl like the wind,
roll like the ocean.
Your mood will be better
when your body's in motion.

But there still might not be
a smile on your face.
There's more work to do
so let's slow down the pace.

First close your eyes,
then give yourself a hug.
Wrap your arms around you
and hold your body snug.

Now open your eyes,
stretch your arms out wide.
First reach to the left
then the right side.

Take a deep breath in,
clench your fists real tight.
Raise your shoulders to your ears
and squeeze with all your might.

Hold that pose
and count one, two, three.
Then let your breath out
and shake your body free!

Take another breath in
and when you are ready,
blow the last of your anger
out strong and steady.

Good job, you did it!
Pat yourself on the back!
You took charge of your anger
and you got back on track.

There will be a next time
when you're feeling this way.
So just remember this rhyme
and have a happier day!

Note to Parents and Caregivers

Many children may feel as though they are not allowed to be angry. However, *A Feel Better Book for Little Tempers* shares a different message with its young readers—it's okay to get mad, if you know what to do. While anger is a natural and healthy emotion, children are often impulsive and lack the self-control to rationally handle disappointing or frustrating situations, therefore their feelings are displayed with temper tantrums, hitting, or other inappropriate but developmentally normal behaviors. Saying "calm down!" or "don't do that!" is a natural response when this happens, but then children may bottle up their feelings instead of trying to cope with and resolve them. This book offers a gentle outlet for these intense or aggressive outbursts of emotion, and verse by verse takes children through the process of identifying, normalizing and most importantly, managing anger in a safe and effective way.

Learning About Anger

While anger is usually an obvious emotion, it is also quite complex. Helping your child learn about anger—how it feels and why it happens—is an important first step in managing tempers.

Recognizing anger. *You're huffy and puffy and just plain not good.* You can help your child learn about anger by labeling the emotion as it happens. For example, if a child routinely throws a tantrum when a younger sibling takes his toy, put his feelings into words by saying "It makes you really angry when your brother takes your toy. I can see you don't like it when he does that!" By calling attention to these emotions, the child can not only identify his feelings as anger, but eventually can learn to communicate when he is angry before those feelings escalate into a tantrum. Furthermore, it's important to address the child's feelings, whether you feel they are justified or not. A simple acknowledgment, "You're disappointed we can't have ice cream for lunch today," helps

a child understand where his anger is coming from. Even if it seems totally unreasonable, the child is still entitled to his opinion about it. Sometimes labeling and acknowledging the feeling actually deescalates strong reactions by showing that you hear what he is saying and are not just blowing him off.

Body awareness. *Now your ears are quite hot and your cheeks are all red.* Anger is typically easy to identify when it is being displayed physically. It is trickier, especially for a child, to recognize those feelings on the inside before they manifest outwardly. Caregivers can help a child develop body awareness to aid in anticipating and recognizing anger. Ask your child how her body feels as the tantrum first starts to happen. "Do you feel hot or stormy inside? What does it feel like inside your body when you're mad like this?"

Defining a temper. *A temper is what happens when your anger's the worst.* Like adults, children will experience anger in varying degrees. To illustrate this concept, you can use a 1–10 rating system. Here's an example: "I see you are angry about that. Let's say 1 means you are only a little angry and 10 means you are SUPER angry! Which number do you feel you are right now?" There's a pretty good chance the child will be a 10 quite often, especially in the beginning. Even if you do not agree, it's important to acknowledge how angry she must feel. After doing this a few times, the child may begin to differentiate between the different levels and give you a wider range of numbers.

Displaying anger. *But you just get in trouble when you bite or you hit.* It's completely normal for children to show their anger physically, but children often don't know what the acceptable boundaries are, or they have not yet developed the self-control to stay within those boundaries. Even though it is absolutely acceptable to feel angry, when a child acts out physically it is important to set limits. You can still acknowledge their feelings, then proceed with giving alternative methods for processing their anger. Setting consistent limits in a firm but gentle way will help regulate the emotions of an otherwise agitated child.

Normalizing. *Even grownups get cranky!* It's important for kids to know that anger is a normal, healthy emotion that everyone feels sometimes, even grownups. Letting your child know when you or someone else is angry allows him to not only recognize that it happens to others too, but also allows him to feel empathy for others.

Tools for Managing Anger

Once children can recognize and accept anger, they just need to learn the tools to safely and effectively manage it.

A safe outlet for anger. *It's okay to get mad if you know what to do.* Children don't always have the capability to calmly manage big emotions in times of stress, and it's unfair to expect differently. Adults must teach children new ways to safely and appropriately express anger. First, label the child's feeling to help her understand what she is feeling with a statement such as: "I know you're mad at your sister. You do not like it when she makes that face at you!" Then proceed with a boundary: "But she is not for pushing." Then give some other choices: "You can squeeze your fists real tight while you take a deep breath in, and then let it all out. That may help with your frustrations. Or you can go outside and do some jumping jacks if you feel you have angry energy inside your body." Remaining calm when things get intense will help deescalate the situation faster. As is usually the case, modeling the appropriate behavior is the best way to demonstrate what to do. This isn't always easy when your own temper is at play, so remember the strategies outlined in the book—they can help you, too!

Mind and body integration. *Pretend your anger is the ball and your arms are the bat.* When children visualize what has made them angry, "slamming" it and "sending that anger far, far away" will feel satisfying. As long as it's safe, exerting angry energy in a physical way allows a person to feel like they are in control—that they were able to do something about the situation.

Empowerment. *Now you have more power and your anger has less.* When someone feels angry, he or she might feel a loss of control. Empowering your child with the knowledge and strategies in this book will allow her to have control over how she responds to the anger, even if she doesn't always have control over the situation.

Movement. *Whirl like the wind, roll like the ocean.* Movement and exercise are proven to help people feel better no matter what emotion they're feeling, whether it's anxiety, sadness, or anger. So don't let children just sit there and stew. Get up and get moving to express those angry feelings! Or go outside and breathe some fresh air—sometimes just changing the scenery can help.

Muscle relaxation. *Squeeze with all your might.* Tensing and relaxing different parts of the body is a technique used in many situations to increase circulation and relaxation. It's also a really safe way to physically work through angry feelings. The book includes a few examples, but caregivers can take it a step further by asking the child to lay on the floor and curl his body in a tight ball. Count with him slowly to five, then ask him to stretch his body out long in all directions. This can be repeated several times. It works even better if caregivers join in on this activity!

Deep breathing. *Blow the last of your anger out.* Strong emotions such as anger can cause physical changes in the body that might actually make symptoms feel worse. Teaching children to take long, deep breaths allows them to take in more oxygen and to slow their heartbeat. One method for helping young children learn to take deep breaths is to pretend they are smelling a candle (in through your nose), then blowing it gently out (out through your mouth). You can also teach children to take deep belly breaths by asking them to lay down and place a small item, such as a toy, on their belly. They can watch the toy move slowly up and down as their breath moves in and out.

Encouragement. *Pat yourself on the back.* Handling anger appropriately can be difficult for adults, so imagine how tough it is for a child whose brain is still in the fundamental stages of development. Even if they do not always get it right, their effort is to be applauded.

A Final Thought

While this book is aimed at giving caregivers simple and effective tools to use at home, in school, or as a clinical supplement, a parent or caregiver should seek additional help if they feel it is necessary. It's important to note that while anger is a natural emotion, excess or uncontrollable anger may require professional guidance. Your child's pediatrician can provide a list of licensed mental health professional referrals.

About the Authors

Sisters LEAH BOWEN and HOLLY BROCHMANN are dedicated wives, mothers, and authors, each passionate about contributing to a mentally healthier society in a meaningful way. Leah has a master of education degree in counseling with a focus in play therapy. She is a licensed professional counselor and registered play therapist in the state of Texas where she currently practices, and she is committed to helping her child clients work through issues including trauma, depression, and anxiety. Holly has a degree in journalism and enjoys creative writing both as a hobby and as a primary part of her career in public relations. This is the sisters' second book in the Feel Better Books for Little Kids series published by Magination Press. The first book, *A Feel Better Book for Little Worriers*, was released in 2017.

About the Illustrator

SHIRLEY NG-BENITEZ loves to draw! Nature, family, and fond memories of her youth inspire her mixed media illustrations. Since '98, she's owned gabbyandco.com, designing, illustrating, and lettering for the technology, greeting card, medical, toy, and publishing industries. She's living her dream, illustrating and writing picture books in San Martin, CA, with her husband, daughters, and pup. Shirley is honored to have illustrated this book as well as *A Feel Better Book for Little Worriers*, also by Holly Brochmann and Leah Bowen and published by Magination Press. You can find more of her work on her website, www.shirleyngbenitez.com

About Magination Press

MAGINATION PRESS is an imprint of the American Psychological Association, the largest scientific and professional organization representing psychologists in the United States and the largest association of psychologists worldwide.